U0022223

For Gemk,

Whose endless supply of ideas and honest critique made this possible.

感謝 Gemk

源源不絕的靈感及誠懇的建議讓這一切成真。

The Ice Sculpture Competition

意外的冰雕比賽

Coleen Reddy 著

沈 斌 繪

薛慧儀 譯

三民書局

Every year in winter, the students at Iris's school have a competition.
It is an Ice Sculpture Competition.
Everyone has to make an ice sculpture.
The prize for the best ice sculpture is $200.

每年冬天，愛瑞絲的學校都會舉行冰雕比賽。
每一個人都要做一座冰雕。
最棒的冰雕可以得到兩百元的獎金喔！

Last year, Iris won the first prize and she wants to win it this year, too.
But it's not going to be easy.
There's a new girl, Irene, who's really good at making ice sculptures.

愛瑞絲去年就得到第一名，今年她還想拿第一名。
但這可不是件容易的事，因為有個新來的女孩艾琳，
她可是個冰雕高手呢！

The competition starts.
Everyone has the whole day to work on their sculptures at school.
The next morning, all the judges will decide who gets the first prize.

比賽開始了！
每個人都有一整天的時間，可以在學校裡刻冰雕。
第二天早上，裁判們會來評定誰是第一名。

Iris is making a castle.
She works very hard and doesn't take a break.
She is sure that her sculpture will be the best.

愛瑞絲雕的是一座城堡。
她刻得很認真，連休息一下都不肯。
她相信自己的冰雕絕對是最棒的！

Suddenly, she hears the other students saying, "Ooh!" and "Aah!"
She looks up and sees a crowd around Irene's table.
She takes a look.

突然，她聽見其他的同學發出「喔！」和「哇啊！」的讚嘆聲。
她抬起頭，看見一群人圍著艾琳的桌子。
於是她也跑過去看看。

Irene's sculpture is amazing.
She has made two dolphins swimming in the sea.
The teacher says, "Wow, Irene, that's really good."

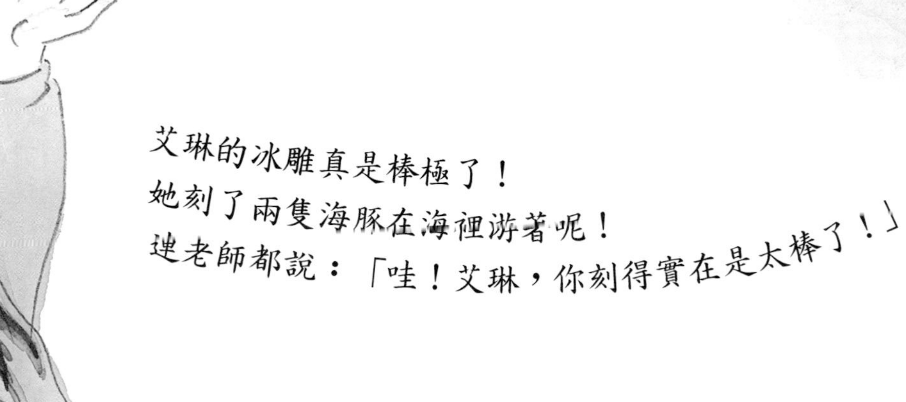

艾琳的冰雕真是棒極了！
她刻了兩隻海豚在海裡游著呢！
連老師都說：「哇！艾琳，你刻得實在是太棒了！」

Iris is so jealous.

She doesn't want Irene to win the first prize.

She will have to do something. She is going to cheat.

愛瑞絲嫉妒得不得了。
她可不想讓艾琳拿到第一名啊！
她得想點辦法才行。
她決定要作弊。

Iris waits until everyone has gone home.
Then, she picks up a knife and starts hacking
away at Irene's ice sculpture.
She uses all her strength.

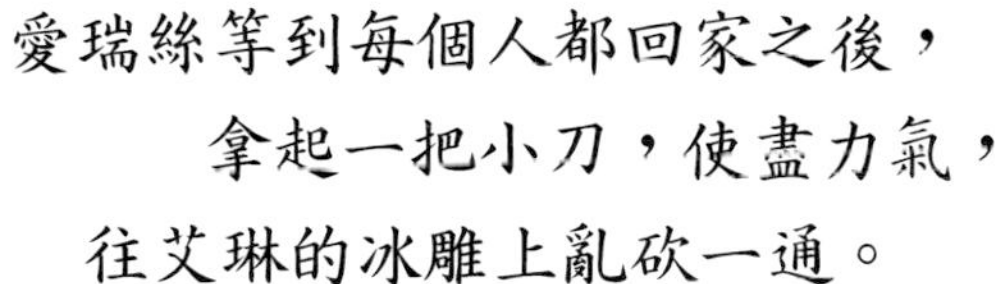

愛瑞絲等到每個人都回家之後，
拿起一把小刀，使盡力氣，
往艾琳的冰雕上亂砍一通。

She stops after some time.
She has completely destroyed Irene's dolphins.
She laughs to herself. Irene will never win now.

過了一會兒，她停了下來。
艾琳的海豚已經完全被她毀了！
她滿意地笑了起來。這下艾琳絕對贏不了她啦！

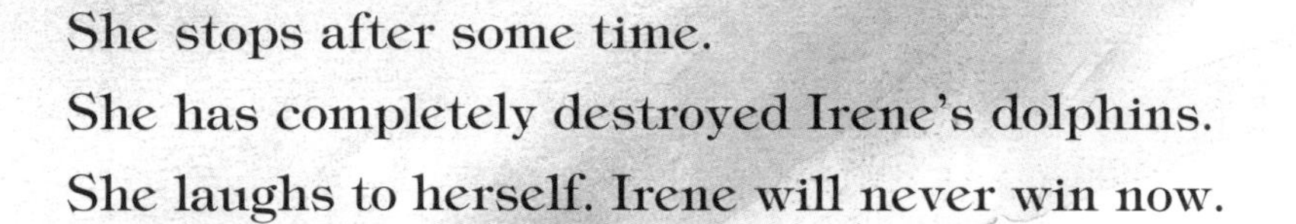

The next day, everyone is excited because
the judges will decide who the winner is.
The judges walk in and everyone follows them.
When Irene sees her ice sculpture, she starts crying.

第二天大家都很興奮，因為裁判將會決定誰是第一名。
裁判走進來了，大家都跟在裁判後面。
艾琳一見到她的冰雕，馬上就哭了起來。

The judges look at Iris's ice sculpture.
"It's good," they whisper. "Let's give her 98."
Iris is so happy. She's going to win.
What will she do with $200?

裁判看了看愛瑞絲的冰雕。

「嗯，真不錯呢！」他們交頭接耳地說。「給她九十八分吧！」

愛瑞絲好高興呀！她就要贏了呢！

該怎麼花這筆兩百元的獎金呢？

But then the judges see Irene's sculpture.
They do not say anything.
They just look at it for some time.
They are not smiling or frowning.

但後來裁判看到艾琳的冰雕時，
他們一句話都沒有說，
只是盯著冰雕看了好一陣子，
既沒有笑，也沒有皺眉頭。

“This is incredible!” says one judge.

“What are they talking about?” thinks Iris. “I destroyed the dolphins.”

“Yes,” says another. “It’s so creative and interesting.
It shows good imagination.”

「這真是太不可思議了！」一個裁判說。

「他們在說什麼呀？」愛瑞絲想。「我把海豚給毀了呀！」

「沒錯！」另一個裁判說。「這件作品極富創造力及趣味，表現了非常豐富的想像力！」

"What is it?" asks Iris loudly.
It is just a blob of ice.
"It can be anything," says the judge.

「那你們覺得這件作品像什麼呀？」愛瑞絲大聲地問。
它只不過是一堆冰塊碎片嘛！
「它可以是任何東西呀！」裁判說。

"It's a great idea," explains the judge. "Because everyone can see it in their own way. For me, it's something sad. Look at the way it lies there. It is saying, 'Look at me. I am sad.'"

"To me," says another judge, "it is a bird that has broken its wings and can't fly."

「這是個很棒的主意！」裁判解釋著。「因為每個人都可以用自己的方法來看這件作品。對我來說，這是一件悲傷的作品，看看這堆碎片躺在地上的模樣，彷彿在說：『你看，我是多麼悲傷呀！』」

「對我而言，」另一個裁判說，「這是一隻斷了翅膀而無法飛翔的鳥兒。」

Are they crazy? A sad blob? A bird with broken wings?
It's nothing!
Iris watches in disbelief as the judges give Irene 100.
Irene wins the prize after all.
Iris's cheating has backfired!

他們的腦袋有沒有問題呀？悲傷的碎片？斷了翅膀的鳥兒？
它根本什麼都不是嘛！
愛瑞絲不敢相信，眼睜睜地看著裁判給了這件作品一百分！
艾琳最後還是贏了這場比賽。
愛瑞絲的作弊行為帶來了反效果！

小小刻畫家

工具與材料

1. 西卡紙　　3. 牙籤
2. 粉蠟筆　　4. 紙膠帶

小朋友，首先要請你動動聰明的小腦袋兒，想想你要刻畫什麼樣的東西，想好了之後，就讓我們一起來動手做！

＊在做勞作之前，要記得在桌上先鋪一張紙或墊板，才不會把桌面弄得髒兮兮喔！

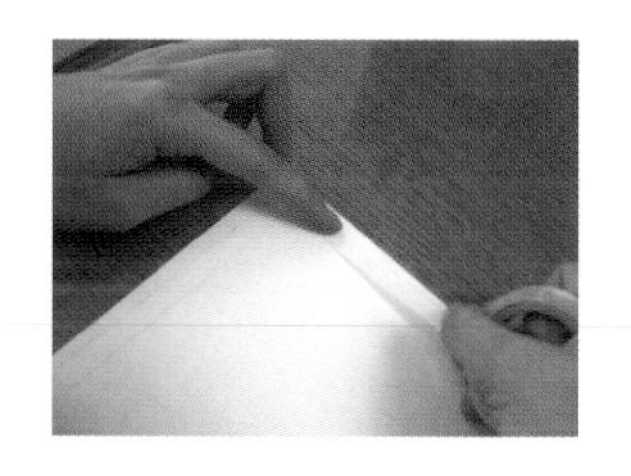

步驟

1. 在西卡紙周圍貼上紙膠帶。
2. 用黑色以外的粉蠟筆在西卡紙上塗色，可以多用幾種不同的顏色，刻出來的圖才會漂亮喔。
3. 等粉蠟筆稍乾之後，再塗上一層黑色粉蠟筆。記得要把下面的顏色蓋掉，並塗滿整張紙。
4. 塗好之後，按照你自己構思的圖案，在西卡紙上面用牙籤刻出來。

生字表

p. 2

competition [ˌkɑmpə`tɪʃən] 名 競爭，比賽

sculpture [`skʌlptʃɚ] 名 雕刻品

prize [praɪz] 名 獎金；獎品

p. 13

amazing [ə`mezɪŋ] 形 令人驚異的

p. 17

hack [hæk] 動 猛砍，劈

strength [strɛŋθ] 名 力量；力氣

p. 18

destroy [dɪ`strɔɪ] 動 破壞；毀壞

p. 22

whisper [`hwɪspɚ] 動 小聲說話

p. 24

frown [fraʊn] 動 皺眉頭

p. 26

incredible [ɪn`krɛdəbl̩] 形 不可思議的

imagination [ɪˌmædʒə`neʃən] 名 想像力

p. 28

blob [blɑb] 名 小圓塊

p. 32

disbelief [ˌdɪsbə`lif] 名 不相信，懷疑

backfire [`bækˌfaɪr] 動 招致相反的效果

中高級・中英對照
探索英文叢書

波波唸翻天系列

你知道可愛的小兔子也會“碎碎唸”嗎？
波波就是這樣。
他將要告訴我們什麼有趣的故事呢？

波波的復活節／波波的西部冒險記／波波上課記／我愛你，波波
波波的下雪天／波波郊遊去／波波打球記／聖誕快樂，波波／波波的萬聖夜

共9本，每本均附CD

國家圖書館出版品預行編目資料

The Ice Sculpture Competition:意外的冰雕比賽 / Coleen Reddy著; 沈斌繪; 薛慧儀譯.－－初版一刷.－－臺北市；三民，2003
面； 公分－－(愛閱雙語叢書. 二十六個妙朋友系列) 中英對照
ISBN 957-14-3770-0 (精裝)
1. 英國語言－讀本
523.38 92008835

© The Ice Sculpture Competition
——意外的冰雕比賽

著作人 Coleen Reddy
繪 圖 沈 斌
譯 者 薛慧儀
發行人 劉振強
著作財產權人 三民書局股份有限公司
臺北市復興北路386號
發行所 三民書局股份有限公司
地址／臺北市復興北路386號
電話／(02)25006600
郵撥／0009998-5
印刷所 三民書局股份有限公司
門市部 復北店／臺北市復興北路386號
重南店／臺北市重慶南路一段61號
初版一刷 2003年7月
編 號 S 85642-1
定 價 新臺幣壹佰捌拾元整
行政院新聞局登記證局版臺業字第○二○○號

有著作權・不准侵害

ISBN 957-14-3770-0 (精裝)